THANK YOU FOR ME!

By **Marion Dane Bauer**

Illustrated by **Kristina Stephenson**

Simon & Schuster Books for Young Readers

NEW YORK   LONDON   TORONTO   SYDNEY

I have two hands
to fold.
I have two hands
to hold,
to clap,
to flap,
to tap.

I have two feet
    that dart,
        that dash,

that sprint,
    that splash.

I have two eyes to see my mama's face,
to see my bear,
to see that paintbrush over there.

The one that says, "Come try me.
There's a picture inside me."

I have two ears
to hear the rush of wind,
the gush of rain,
the thunder's *boom-a-room,*
room-a-boom.

To hear my daddy's
"Hush-sh-sh-sh!"

I have one nose.
It pokes right out.

It's not a beak.
It's not a snout.

My nose smells rain,
my puppy's fur,

Grandpa's bread,
or his roses instead.

I have one mouth
with tongue and teeth,

a nose above,

a chin beneath.

I sing.
I talk.

I smile.
I eat.

Apples, crisp and sweet,
peanut butter, drumsticks,
long, long licks of chocolate ice cream.

I have this skin.
It's nice and tight.
See how it fits
exactly right?

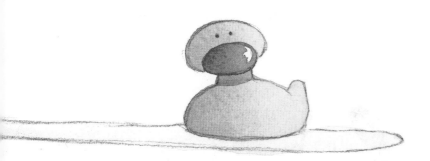

I have one body

to stretch, to curl,

to bounce, to twirl.

I have two hands to pray.
I have one heart to listen.
I have one mouth to say . . .
Thank you!

Thank you for hands and feet
that keep a beat,

for ears that hear,
and eyes that see.
Thank you for each bendy knee.

Thank you for my mouth that eats
meat and vegetables and treats,

for fingers and toes,
and for my nose.
Thank you for the way
every bit of me grows.

Thank you for the skin I came in,
and for my body so fine.
It's all mine!

Thank you for me!

To Chester, who fills us all with gratitude—M. D. B.
For Olivia and Oscar Found with lots of love—K. S.

SIMON & SCHUSTER BOOKS FOR YOUNG READERS
An imprint of Simon & Schuster Children's Publishing Division
1230 Avenue of the Americas, New York, New York 10020
Text copyright © 2010 by Marion Dane Bauer
Illustrations copyright © 2010 by Kristina Stephenson
All rights reserved, including the right of reproduction in whole or in part in any form.
SIMON & SCHUSTER BOOKS FOR YOUNG READERS is a trademark of Simon & Schuster, Inc.
For information about special discounts for bulk purchases, please contact
Simon & Schuster Special Sales at 1-866-506-1949 or business@simonandschuster.com.
The Simon & Schuster Speakers Bureau can bring authors to your live event.
For more information or to book an event, contact the Simon & Schuster Speakers Bureau at
1-866-248-3049 or visit our website at www.simonspeakers.com.
Book design by Chloë Foglia
The text for this book is set in Barcelona.
The illustrations for this book were inspired by Kristina's children, sketched out in pencil and painted
(to music, of course) in Tube Watercolors on Arches Cold Pressed Watercolor Paper.
Manufactured in China
2 4 6 8 10 9 7 5 3 1
Library of Congress Cataloging-in-Publication Data
Bauer, Marion Dane.
Thank you for me / Marion Dane Bauer ; illustrated by Kristina Stephenson.—1st ed.
p. cm.
Summary: Rhythmic text enumerates what various body parts can do,
including hands to clap and a body to twirl, then express thanks for each of those parts—and the whole.
ISBN 978-0-689-85788-1
(1. Body, Human—Fiction. 2. Gratitude—Fiction.) I. Stephenson, Kristina, ill. II. Title.
PZ7.B3262Tha 2010
(E)—dc22
2006023872